majikkids

Magical Stories for Magical Kids!

Fairtrade Publishing

Majik Kids is the first ever Fair Trade Publishing company. We value the artists we work with, and pay them 50% of the revenue we generate from book sales. When you buy our books or subscription, you support these hard-working, creative humans to inspire your kids. Thank you for your support!

Bradley T. Morris

"A big thank you to my wife, Celeste for supporting me to pursue my passion and
love for golf by playing almost every day at sunrise — in every weather imaginable!"

Céline Sawchuk

"I dedicate this story to all the big and little kids out there!
Dream big, believe in yourself and never give up!"

ISBN: 978-1-990568-27-5 (Paperback)
ISBN: 978-1-990568-28-2 (E-Book)

The characters in this book are entirely fictional. Any resemblance to actual persons living or dead is entirely
coincidental. Names, characters, and places are products of the author's imagination.

Written By: Bradley T. Morris
Illustrated By: Céline Sawchuk
Book Design By: Céline Sawchuk
Edited By: Courtney Shepard

Printed by IngramSpark, Inc., in the United States of America.
First printing edition 2022
IngramSpark 14 Ingram Blvd, La Vergne, TN 37086, United States

www.MajikKids.com

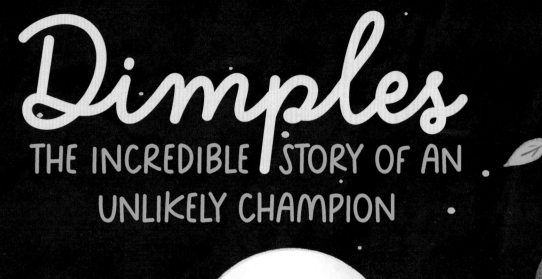

Dimples
THE INCREDIBLE STORY OF AN UNLIKELY CHAMPION

WRITTEN BY: BRADLEY T. MORRIS + SAURYN MAJIK
ILLUSTRATED BY: CELINE SAWCHUK

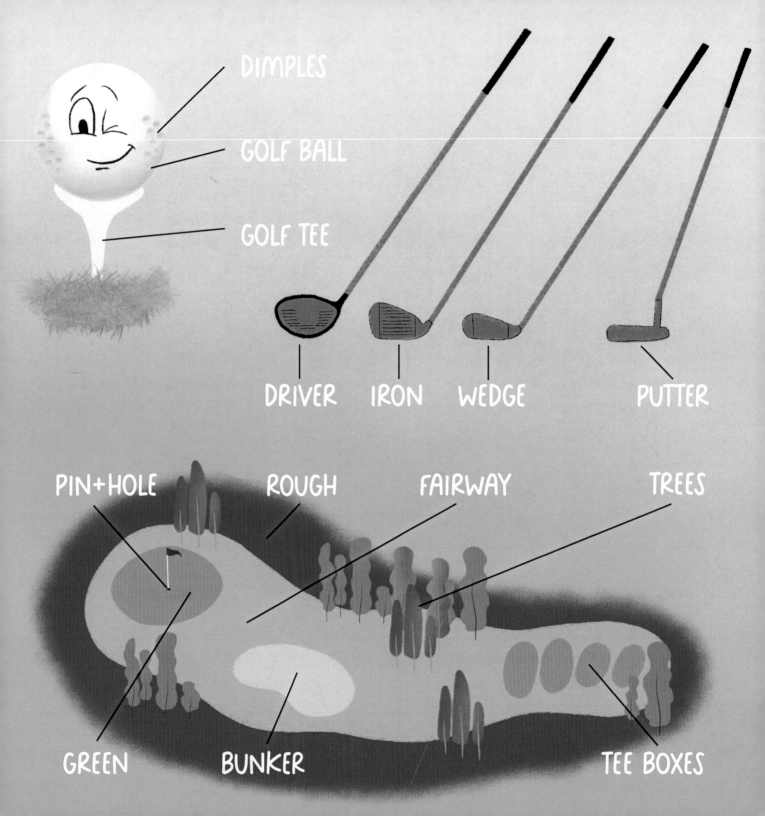

Hello! My name is Dimples, and I am a Golf ball.

I know, I know – you're probably thinking to yourself, "What!? A story being told by a Golf ball?!" That's right! And it's quite an incredible and inspiring story, too.
But before I get into it, I just have to tell you a few things about this wonderful game called, Golf – just in case you're new to the sport.

Golf is a long-honored sport played outside on a beautiful expanse of grass called a Golf course. The goal of Golf is to hit a little ball (like me!) into a little hole with a tool called a Golf club (see diagram!). The problem is, the hole is hundreds of yards away, and there are often obstacles in the way, like ponds or trees or pits of sand, called hazards. What makes it even more difficult is that the hole is very small! You start each hole at a tee box, where you balance your ball on a little white stick called a tee. You want to hit your ball into the fairway, which is the short grass down the middle. The rough is the longer grass that lines both sides of the fairway.

The green is the really, really short grass with the little hole and a flagstick that is stuck inside it, so you know where the hole is from far away. You want to hit the ball onto the green and into the hole in as few shots as possible.

-4	CONDOR	FOUR STROKES UNDER PAR
-3	ALBATROSS	THREE STROKES UNDER PAR
-2	EAGLE	TWO STROKES UNDER PAR
-1	BIRDIE	ONE STROKE UNDER PAR
E	PAR	EQUAL TO PAR
+1	BOGEY	ONE STROKE OVER PAR
+2	DOUBLE BOGEY	TWO STROKES OVER PAR
+3	TRIPLE BOGEY	THREE STROKES OVER PAR
+4	QUADRUPLE BOGEY	FOUR STROKES OVER PAR

18

THE LAST HOORAH

PAR 4

415
390
370

In a full game of golf, there are 18 different holes. The goal for each hole is to "make par."
To make par, using your Golf club, you must hit the ball into the hole in the correct number of strokes (also known as shots). For instance, if it's a "par 4," your goal is to get your ball in the hole with just four shots.

If you get the ball in the hole in one shot under par (like say it only takes you three strokes on a par four), then that's called a birdie. Birdies are good!

If it takes an extra shot to get the ball in the hole (like, say, it takes five shots on a par four), then that's called a bogey (which almost sounds like a booger!).
Obviously, it's better to get birdies than boogers... I mean bogeys.

If you get the ball in the hole in two shots under par (like only two shots on a par 4), then that's called an eagle. Those are awesome!

If it takes you two extra shots more than par to get the ball in the hole, that's called a (you guessed it) DOUBLE BOGEY. Those aren't so great.

The last thing I will say is that there is no better feeling than hitting a perfectly struck golf shot. It's like magic.
Now that we have the formalities out of the way – let's get onto the story!

Most Golf balls dream of being a champion, but not all of us are lucky enough to become one. My journey began where all Golf ball journeys begin, the place where I was created, in a factory. My creators were a team of lab coat-wearing engineers and robotic arms who consciously placed each of the geometrically designed dimples on my face – allowing for ultimate aerodynamics in flight. I still remember the feeling when the "brand stamper machine" pressed my logo on my forehead. I felt as though I was the chosen one.

At least until I looked around and realized that there were more than a million other Golf balls made on that very same day. Unfortunately, not all of us would become champions. Many-a-ball's fate would end up in a hazard, like a lake or a pond, lost and forgotten forever.

Yes, very few of us would one day get to sit upon a trophy shelf – like the one I now call my throne. The euphoria of having my label pressed upon my head was followed by confusion when I was unceremoniously whisked off the carousel and popped into a tiny box with two other golf balls.

Then they pushed us into a bigger box with three more small boxes of golf balls inside it. And then a lid was placed upon the top and darkness ensued.

It's hard to say how much time passed as we waited in silence in our claustrophobic confines, but it felt like forever. Each of us was hoping, wishing, wanting our chance to be used so that we may fulfill our purpose for being created.

One day I was suddenly blinded by a bright light. I could hear the sound of birds chirping all around me as the lid of my box was lifted. As my eyes adjusted, I felt a sense of awe when I laid my gaze on my golfer.

He was a tall, round, giant of a man with a large honking nose. He had hair growing out of his jumbo ears, and his cheeks glowed a jolly red. His pants were a checkered pattern with bright yellow and black squares, and he wore a shirt that was two sizes too small, barely containing his underbelly. His name was Duff, and he was a thing of beauty. It was my honour and duty to serve Duff in his game of Golf that day.

I was finally able to fulfill my purpose. When his sausage-sized fingers reached into the box and selected me, I felt weightless as I ascended from my cardboard prison.
"You'll do the trick, little ball," he said under his breath as he squiggled a black smiley face upon my cover to mark that I was his and he was mine. He then pulled the longest club from his bag, called a Driver, walked over to the first hole tee box, and placed me on a small wooden tee.

One of his chums gave him some words of encouragement. "Hey Duff, don't hit it in the water, eh?" But Duff was too focused to take note. He dug his feet into the ground, gave his bum and club a waggle or two and then suddenly, he went completely still.

I could tell the moment I had been waiting for my entire life was about to arrive.

Duff brought his club back and swung as hard as he possibly could. I closed my eyes, waiting for the moment of impact, but nothing more than a gust of wind hit me when his club passed by my head. All of his buddies exploded into laughter. "That counts as a shot!" they said between uncontrollable giggles.

Because in Golf, if you intend to hit the ball and miss, it still counts as a shot or a stroke. "Hey, that was a practice swing!" Duff argued. And without waiting another second, he swung again and SMASHED me, right in the forehead, sending me flying a foot or two off the ground. I swear I saw some worms duck out of the way as I flew by... but I was out of control and sailed straight into the pond down the right side of the fairway. I skipped across the water three times, and just when I thought I would make it across to dry land, I hit a rock, and it sent me flying backwards. I landed right in the water. SPLASH!

"Nooooo!" I gurgled as I floated down to the bottom of the pond, settling three feet from the surface. Eventually, I spotted Duff standing at the pond's edge, but it seemed he didn't see me because he reached into his pocket, dropped another ball, and called out to his friends, "I found it! It must've hit a rock!"

"That's not the right ball!" I gurgled to Duff. But it was no use. He hit the new ball and disappeared out of sight. Could that be it? My destiny – done? Was one shot all I got?

Duff never came back for me. In fact, nobody did. Fall turned to winter. The pond froze. I watched skaters play hockey overhead. Eventually, the ice melted... but the sadness in my heart remained. The aloneness I felt at the bottom of that first hole pond was greater than I can explain. "Is one shot all I've got in me?" I wondered as the months dragged by.

But just like before, one unsuspecting day, my luck changed. A strange-looking pole came plunging into the water, with a little cup on the end of it. Suddenly, I was plucked up from the muddy bottom and brought back to the surface, where I could breathe again. I stared up at an older man with caterpillar eyebrows. He looked at me through his spectacles with adoration.

"Ophelia will love you," he cheerfully said to himself.
I didn't know what an "Ophelia" was, but I was grateful someone found me.

Suddenly, I was plopped into the bucket he was carrying alongside 80 to 100 other muddy Golf balls. The elderly man was named Mulligan and he enjoyed collecting Golf balls, polishing them up and reselling them in egg cartons at the end of his laneway. But for some reason, he took a liking to me and wanted to give me to somebody special. That somebody special was his granddaughter Ophelia.

Mulligan was going to visit her because she was playing in her first big junior Golf tournament at the Majik Oaks Golf Club, and he would be her caddie, which is every golfer's best friend.

A caddie carries your bag, offers advice, and encourages you when you need it most.

After scrubbing me up, Mulligan put me in his pocket, and off we went for a long car ride.

When we got to Ophelia's home, it was dark out. I heard a young girl's excited voice from outside the car, "YAY! It's Grandpa Mulligan!"

The door opened, and Grandpa Mulligan greeted his granddaughter, "Ophelia, my girl. So nice to see you. I found you something special." "What is it?" she energetically questioned. He pulled me out of his jacket pocket and placed me in her open hand. "I thought the smiley face would be a good reminder to have fun tomorrow at the big tournament. It's pretty much a brand-new ball. Looks like it was only hit once."

I felt nervous as I stared up into her olive eyes, looking back down at me. Would she like me? Would she choose to use a different Golf ball? I waited with bated breath. Finally, after an eternity passed, she squealed, "I love it! It's my lucky ball for the big tournament. Thank you, Grandpa Mulligan!"

"So, are you feeling ready?" Grandpa Mulligan curiously questioned.

"I feel a bit scared but also excited," Ophelia replied shyly. "You'll do just fine, Ophelia. Show up and play the best you can on each shot. It's all we can do in life," Grandpa replied thoughtfully.

Ophelia was scheduled to tee off early the following day, so we went straight to bed after we got inside the House. Ophelia planted a kiss on me before setting me on her bedside table and falling asleep. I didn't sleep a wink that night.

The next morning, we got to the course with plenty of time to warm up. Watching Ophelia hit balls on the driving range before her round was mesmerizing. Her swing was graceful and pure. She made solid contact most of the time. I couldn't wait to feel her club hit me in the face out on the course.

When she got to the practice putting green to roll some putts, she used me as her practice ball. Ophelia took me from her pocket, polished me on her shirt, and said, "It's a big day today, Dimples." "Dimples?" It was the first time I ever heard my name. I loved it!

I couldn't shake the nerves, and so we missed the first few putts. "Be calm. Focus." Ophelia reminded me under her breath. "Right!" I whispered back. "Relax."

I let myself relax, and with the next few putts, we hit on our intended line. The first time I fell into the hole felt like coming home. "Ahh, this is what I'm supposed to do!" It was exhilarating to hit the bottom of the cup. It made the most incredible sound I have ever heard. PLUNK! I wanted to do it again and again.

Finally, our time came to go to the first tee. Ophelia and I were the first to hit in her group. Looking out at our first shot, I felt a sudden surge of anxiety. Ophelia had to hit me over a big pond. I felt myself freezing up.

I couldn't stop thinking about my last Golf shot and how lonely I felt after being lost. Ophelia was nervous too. Her hands were slightly shaking as she tried to place me on her tee. Remember to breathe, feel your feet, and have fun," Grandpa Mulligan gently reminded Ophelia before giving her the driver. I let out a deep sigh of relief and stared up at her as she settled in to hit.

I can't even describe the intensity of that first shot. She wound up and absolutely crushed me down the middle. I sailed over the pond. "YAHOO!!!" I shouted.

And then I landed right in the middle of the fairway. Ophelia used her 9 iron, hitting me from the fairway, and I landed ten feet from the cup. "Way to go!" Grandpa Mulligan cheered.

Her putt was a downhill slider, and I didn't lean quite hard enough, causing me to slip past the cup by two feet, missing our birdie opportunity. She tapped me in, and we had a par on the first hole. It felt great. I played an entire hole without getting lost! I couldn't wait for the rest of the day.

The second hole was a par 3. We stood on the tee, feeling a gentle breeze blowing into our faces. Even though Ophelia hit her 6 iron well, the wind pushed me left of the green, and I bounced down into a deep sand trap – also known as a bunker. She was upset with herself, but not for long because Grandpa Mulligan offered her some words of encouragement. "Golf is a game of misses, Ophelia. Whoever misses their shots the best will win. Don't let one little miss get you down."

She smiled, took a deep breath, and said, "Okay, Grandpa." Ophelia used her wedge to fly me right onto the green. I landed hard and fast and tried my best to lean and hit the flagstick to slow down. "CLANK!" I bounced off the flag and stopped two feet from the pin. "What a shot, Ophelia!" called Grandpa Mulligan from up on the green.

I felt both relieved and proud as Ophelia tapped me into the hole and saved our par. We walked to the next hole feeling a great sense of relief. The next few holes were a bit of a blur. It took everything I had in me to stay focused on the present moment and shot at hand. I couldn't help but want to know how other players were doing. I wondered what we would need to shoot in order to win. Ophelia must have been wondering the same thing because as we walked up to the third tee, Grandpa Mulligan quietly reminded Ophelia while handing her the driver: "We still have a lot of golf in front of us today, Ophelia. Let's focus all your energy on the next shot we must take. The birdies will eventually come if we're patient."

It seemed this idea of letting things come to us helped us both relax. We made three more pars in a row. But on hole six, I got stuck in the mud in a little creek in front of the green. I thought I was a goner, and Ophelia would drop another ball. But she didn't. She kept her cool, took off her shoes, and squished through the mud, hitting me up onto the green. "SPLAT!" Dirt went flying, and so did I.

We missed our par save and walked away with a disappointing bogey. As we sat on a bench at the 7th tee, we must have looked pretty down because Grandpa Mulligan caught Ophelia's gaze and reminded her, "It's about how you react to bad holes and heavy emotions. Are you going to allow them to take you down a negative spiral, or are you going to let them fuel you to play better? Lift your head and stand tall. You hit a courageous shot back there. Let's refocus and try to have some fun!"

Ophelia and I smiled, recognizing that we were still in this tournament. We couldn't let a bogey get us down. Grandpa Mulligan's motivational pep talk worked wonders because Ophelia stepped up and made three birdies in a row!

You may not believe it, but Ophelia and I were going into the back nine leading the tournament! Was I the same Golf ball who had been lost on my first shot the previous year? Going into the 10th hole, my mind was racing. I started to get ahead of myself, imagining what it would feel like to win this tournament.

I completely left the present moment, and in leaving the present moment, I left Ophelia. "CRACK!" The sound of her club hitting me off the tee snapped me back to reality. The next thing I knew, I landed in the rough and took one big bounce into some tall grass (called fescue), settling beneath an ancient oak tree.

"OPHELIA! I cried. "I'm sorry!" But it was no use. She didn't hear me. Once she got up to the long grass, she only had three minutes to find me before I would be deemed lost. Just before her time expired, I saw the big smile & bushy eyebrows of Grandpa Mulligan peeking down at me. "I found your ball over here, Ophelia!" he called.

She was thrilled, but the excitement turned to anger when she saw how buried I was in the long grass. Just get it back into the fairway, and we'll try to save par from there" Grandpa Mulligan suggested. "No!" said Ophelia, "I'm going to hit this up on the green."

"GULP!" I swallowed. I wanted to encourage Ophelia to listen to Grandpa Mulligan, but the words wouldn't come out. Instead, I witnessed in horror as she took one swing – and missed. A second swing – and missed again. Finally, her third swing chunked down on me, and I came popping up in the air, just barely making it back out onto the fairway. Remember, missing the ball when you intend to hit, counts as a shot in Golf. We had counted four strokes and still were not on the green. Fortunately, Ophelia hit a great shot with her pitching wedge and tapped in her putt for a heartbreaking double bogey.

We fell two shots back from the leader.

FIRST TEE OPEN

Player	Score	Hole
DAEUS	-2	11
SAURYN	-2	13
ANA	-1	12
RUMI	-1	12
OPHELIA	-	11
EDEN	-	17
RAVEN	+1	18
ADDIE	+1	13
COCO	+2	13
KALEV	+2	17

We walked to the 11th tee box in silence. Grandpa Mulligan stayed a few paces behind. I wanted him to say something encouraging, but he just gave Ophelia space to feel what she felt. I later realized how wise this was of him to let her feel her feelings, because we must feel to let go entirely. The 11th hole was a short par 3 over a pond, with sand traps left and right.

Ophelia waited on a bench with her head slumped in her hands while her playing partners hit. When it was her turn, she went to get her pitching wedge from Grandpa Mulligan. But before he handed it over, he said to her, "Remember Ophelia, this is just a game, and a game you love. There are no guarantees in this game, nor are there in life. We just don't know what's going to happen between now and the 18th hole. All you can do is show up with your best attitude, hit your best shots, and try to enjoy yourself out here."

If Golf balls could cry, I swear a tear would have run down my dimples, listening to Grandpa Mulligan's inspirational words. He was right, and Ophelia knew it. "Thanks, Grandpa," Ophelia said. I could feel her relax as I sat gripped in the palm of her hand. She placed me upon the little wooden tee and wasted no time at all.

She stepped up, swung, and absolutely pured me. I flew up into the air and kept my eyes focused on the flag stick below as I sailed down from the sky. I landed on the front of the green and bounced as high as I could, causing me to roll down a little slope and straight towards the flagstick. I was slowing down. I wasn't going to make it.

"Come on, Dimples, go in!" I heard Ophelia call back from the tee box.
"Keep going!" Grandpa Mulligan called.

And just as I thought I would stop on the edge of the cup, I fell forward and dropped down into the hole. Everyone watching cheered. We made a hole-in-one! I couldn't believe it. When Ophelia picked me up from the cup, she planted a big kiss on me.

We had the biggest smiles on our faces, and just like that; we were back in the lead again. In the holes to follow, we were neck-in-neck with the leader, who was one of the older kids in our group. The 12th to the 16th hole was full of zig-zags and gasps and dodging all kinds of hazards...except one.

On the 16th hole, I misjudged how far to carry and landed in a sand trap. Ophelia handed her club to Grandpa Mulligan without a word and began speed-walking towards her ball. She was anxious. "Ophelia," Mulligan called from behind. She stopped and looked back.

"Walk with me, dear. Your ball will still be there when we get there. Let's slow down your steps, slow down your breathing, and take notice of how beautiful this golf course is." Ophelia smiled and slowed her pace. "Okay, Grandpa."

"Do you hear the birds chirping and the crickets singing?" Mulligan asked. "I do,"; Ophelia replied calmly. "It's beautiful!"

They walked the fairway, pointing out their favourite trees to each other, immersed in the moment they were in, and not at all concerned about me up in the bunker. When she arrived at the bunker, Ophelia was noticeably calmer. Even when she spotted me sitting in a terrible position, she didn't react negatively. There was no way Ophelia would be able to hit me to the green. But instead of frowning, she smiled.

"Hi Dimples!" she said cheerfully. "I'm going to hit you out onto the fairway and try to save par from there." "Oh-Oh-Okay." I stammered, surprised to hear how calm she was, given the circumstances.

Ophelia played her best, but we still bogeyed the hole. Her playing partner ended up sinking their par putt, and we fell one shot back from the lead. What a roller coaster ride we were on!
But Ophelia wasn't the slightest bit angry this time. She had a look of calm confidence on her face. Not me, though. I was a nervous wreck, starting to think about losing and that I may never get a chance like this again. The view from the elevated tee box on the 17th hole took my breath away and halted my stinking thinking - otherwise known as negative thoughts.

"Feel your feet planted on the Earth, Ophelia, and send this ball to the moon!"Grandpa Mulligan encouraged her as he handed her the driver. Given how high up we were and how far below the fairway was, it did indeed feel like I might be sent to the moon.

Ophelia's confidence, combined with Mulligan's encouragement, calmed my nerves and brought me back to the present moment. Ophelia looked like a tiger hunting down her prey as she lined up her shot and stepped up to address me with her club. I could see that she was breathing deep, slow, controlled breaths, keeping her nerves as calm as a still pond. I'm not sure what she did to generate more power, whether it was her feet rooted to the ground or the adrenaline of being in contention for the win, but she hit me so hard, so pure, and so straight – SMASH! – I launched off the club face and flew straight for the rising moon off in the distance.

I really thought I might leave the atmosphere, or that my cover may rip off because she struck me so hard. I landed on a hard patch of fairway and flew forward down the sloping hill, and rolled right onto the front edge of the green. I couldn't believe it. We were putting for an Eagle! Ophelia's playing partner, who was currently in the lead, was 30 yards from the green and chipped their ball close, giving themselves an easy two-putt par. This was our chance. If Ophelia made the 30 foot putt, we would be leading by one. She circled the hole like a tiger ready to strike, eyeing up all of the subtle slopes on the green to calculate how hard to hit me and on what line. Once she felt ready, she stepped up and took a couple of practice strokes to figure out how hard to hit me so I would drop into that cup for the eagle. She hit me firmly but on the perfect line. I was heading straight for the cup, but I was going too fast. I needed to slow down, and then – THUD!

I hit the back of the cup, flew straight up into the air, and landed on the rim. Time stood still for a moment. I sat there hovering over the edge of the cup, looking down.

And then suddenly, as if a gentle breeze picked up, I made my final roll and fell-fell-fell into the bottom of the hole. "WHAT AN EAGLE!" Grandpa Mulligan clapped and cheered as he and Ophelia exchanged high fives. I couldn't stop laughing when she came over to pick me up from the hole. "Great putt!" I congratulated. We were all smiling as we stood there on the 18th tee box taking in the beautiful bright pink and orange painted sunset sky.

The incredible symphony of ten thousand frogs beginning to croak suddenly filled our ears. We were now leading the tournament with just one hole to play. I could hardly contain my excitement. But I had to. I needed to stay focused for Ophelia. "Believe in yourself." The voice of Grandpa Mulligan chimed into my thought bubble as he handed Ophelia her 7 iron. The final hole was a downhill par 3 with a lake surrounding most of the green. It was a scary-looking shot from up above where we stood. I would be lying if I said I wasn't scared. Ophelia looked calm, but I was trembling. I didn't want to let her down, but I also didn't want to be hit into the water, where I could spend the rest of my life.

"Breathe and believe," I repeated as the fearful thoughts began creeping in again. As Ophelia set up to hit her tee shot, a sweet moment was exchanged between us. She smiled down at me, and I smiled up at her. It lasted just a moment before she swung, but it made me realize that everything was going to be alright. I just needed to get out of my own way. She swung with perfect tempo and made crisp contact with her club. I launched up into the air and enjoyed the feeling of the wind whipping against my face as I flew towards the green.

I landed on the front right fringe and took a big hop to the left, rolling forward to the middle of the green. It was a perfectly safe shot. We were about 15 feet to the flag. But Ophelia's playing partner was relentless. They hit an 8 iron to two feet from the flag and would have an easy tap in birdie to tie us. Oh gosh, it was all coming down to this final shot. If we missed, we would be forced into a sudden-death playoff hole.

"Send that little ball of yours home," Grandpa Mulligan encouraged when we arrived at the green, handing Ophelia her putter. With our hearts pounding, her palms sweating, and our faces smiling – Ophelia circled the hole once again. As she stood up to hit me, time slowed down. I could hear her heart pounding. I could feel the short grass beneath me. As she tapped me with her putter, I began to roll forward. With each rotation, I moved closer to the hole. It was calling me home. I saw Ophelia raise her club in the air as I approached the cup.

I saw Grandpa Mulligan clasp his hands over his face as his mouth dropped and eyes widened. I caught the right side of the cup and circled all the way around the hole. Everything disappeared and was followed by the sweet sound of success. My favorite sound in the world. The sound of me, a Golf ball, hitting the bottom of the cup. Kerplunk! All of the people standing around the green watching began to cheer. Ophelia ran over to the hole, picked me up, and planted a big kiss on my cheek. "We did it, Dimples. We did it! We won!" I couldn't believe it.

Out of the millions of balls made on the day of my birth, I had done it.

I was a championship-winning Golf ball. I fulfilled my purpose and found my way home.

And so here I am now, sitting on Ophelia's trophy shelf, sharing my story as a reminder to you, that if I can do it, you can do it too. Whether it's in Golf or in life, you were born for greatness. Your success may not come easily. But the hard work, passion, and dedication you pour into your craft and into this game we call life will be worth every ounce of sweat and tears invested.

And most importantly, it's not about whether we win or lose - it's about how much fun we have and the friendships we make along the way.

Breathe deep, feel your feet, and have fun!

Ophelia

The End...

...AND THE BEGINNING!

Join the **majik**kidsclub

fun for the whole family!

Be the first to hear our new stories & meditations, access our downloadable colouring books, get games, activities, cool conversation starters, discounts on books and other magical stuff that's fun for the whole family! Enjoy a sample of what's included in the Majik Kids Club in the following pages.

www.MajikKids.com/Club

Colour the Colouring Book

Find the whole Colouring Book in the Majik Kids Club!

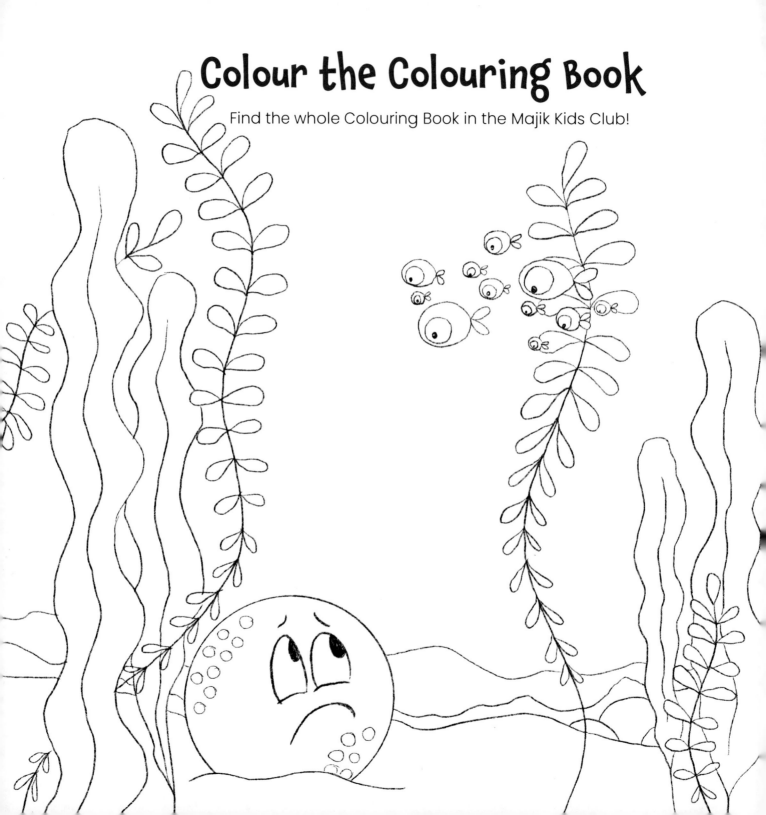

Golf Quiz:

1. If you swing your Golf club with the intent to hit your Golf ball, but miss the ball, does it count as a shot?

a. No

b. Yes

c. Only if the ball moves

d. It depends on who is looking

e. Not if your name is Duff

2. When Dimples is lost in the long grass on hole #10, how long does Ophelia have to find him before he is deemed "Lost?"

a. 1 Minute

b. 3 Minutes

c. 5 Minutes

d. Until she gets bored

e. As long as she wants

3. What do you call the longest Golf club in your bag?

a. Putter

b. Pitching wedge

c. Driver

d. Rake

e. 4-Iron

Draw your Dimples Face

Below is a blank Golf ball. Draw your Dimples face on the Golf ball.

To listen to an audio version of this story and to find many more magical books, join the Majik Kids Club at www.MajikKids.com/Club!

Bradley T. Morris is the founder and creative director of Majik Kids. He is also an extremely passionate golf-lover who plays 250 days per year, in every type of weather imaginable. For fun, he competes professional in his spare time and still has dreams and aspirations of taking a couple years off work to play Pro Golf full time.

Sauryn Majik is an author and creative director at Majik Kids who has co-authored 10 books with his Papa Bear, Bradley as a part of his homeschooling education. He also voice acts and makes up worlds in his imagination. Sauryn hit his first golf shot at the age of 7-months old and giggled his bum off. He goes out on the course with his Papa once or twice per week.

Céline Sawchuk is one of our inhouse graphic designers and the founder of Mind Palace Designs. Immigrating from Germany, she resides on Salt Spring Island, BC, where she finds inspiration in everything around her. She loves playing music and travel and since the beginning of 2020, is a proud mother of a beautiful little boy.